To my beautiful and amazing daughter Kali Love.

Thank you for challenging me and choosing me as your Mommy!

This journey has been epic!

HoneyBee Publishing Co.*
Published in 2023
By HoneyBee Publishing Co.
Katy TX
www.honeybeepublishing.net

Written by Keeyawna Porchè

Illustrated by Noor El Sehnawi

Keeyawna Porchè

Unicorn Dreams

Illustrated by
Noor El Sehnawi

HoneyBee Publishing Co.

Once upon a time, in a far away land, there lived a little girl named, Kali Love.

Kali was 8 years old with golden, sun-kissed skinned that shimmered in the sunlight and long sandy brown locks that bounced up and down when she walked. Kali lived in Katy, Texas which was well known for its mystical star filled skies, tall dancing trees and fairy gardens.

Everyone knew Kali; she had some of the best friends ever! And the most special one of all was her bestie, Dreamy Sugar Sparkles.

Dreamy was the cutest unicorn in all of Katy. They were inseparable. You could always find them playing hide n seek in Kali's tent, cuddled up watching a movie or playing in the backyard. Everyone loved to play with Kali and her bestie, Dreamy and hear all about the fun they always had together.

Even though they spent all of their time together, there was still a secret fairytale experience that Dreamy had not told anyone about, not even her bestie, Kali.

On every Monday of every week, all of the fairytale creatures gather to have a dance battle party. They sit and talk about new TikTok moves, all the latest POP songs and share all the Amazon 'must haves'.

Even though each week comes by so fast, Dreamy treats each Monday like it's unlike any other day. She can't believe it's been a whole week already. And there it was again... just around the corner. Dreamy was excitedly counting the hours and minutes before the dance battle party. She was more than ready to dance all her jitter bugs away and show her friends all the new TikTok challenges she learned.

The dance battle party always happens on the perfect day of the year; the perfect day of the week and fairytale creatures from near and far meet in the secret garden in the middle of the forest. Fairies, unicorns, mermaids and princesses get together for one whole day where all the magic happens.

On Sunday, Kali was playing in the backyard when she overheard Dreamy talking to all the fairytale creatures about the dance battle party planned for tomorrow.

Couldn't believe what she was hearing. Many joyful thoughts ran through Kali's head, so she decided to ask Dreamy if she could join her at this party.

The next day, Kali and Dreamy woke up to the yummy smell of banana pancakes, one of Kali's favorite breakfast foods. When they sat at the table to eat, Kali leaned over and whispered in Dreamy's ear, "Can I come to the fairytale dance battle party with you?" "Of course you can, Kali!" exclaimed Dreamy. "It starts in one hour, so let's go get dressed in our favorite princess dresses." Kali was so excited! She told her mommy and daddy about her BIG day.

After they finished getting ready, Kali and Dreamy ran downstairs to say goodbye to their parents. "Bye, Mommy! Bye, Daddy! See you later," said Kali.

Finally, they were headed to meet the other fairytale creatures in the secret garden. "This is much farther than I thought it would be," said Kali.

"I know," said Dreamy, "but we're almost there. Let's stop here to pick some lemonberries and then finish our walk."

"Okay!" Kali said happily. Lemonberries were one of her favorite fruits. She ate them all the time.

Once they were full, they continued on their journey. When Kali noticed golden sun rays shining across the trees and glistening fairy dust floating in the air, she knew they must be close. With each step, she realized her feet were getting lighter and lighter. "Oh my God! Dreamy, I'm floating, I'm floating!"

Dreamy laughed and said, "Yes, isn't it magical? For some reason we can only float when we're in the secret garden... I guess that's why it's a secret."

Kali couldn't believe what was happening, but there was definitely magic in the air. She loved the secret garden already. They began to float over the shimmery ice- blue lagoon. "What's that?" Kali asked.

"Oh, that's Mermaid Cove. That's where all the mermaids live," Dreamy explained. Kali's eyes grew bigger and bigger in excitement. "I finally get to meet a real live mermaid?" she asked.

"You sure do," said Dreamy. "There's one right there. Hi, Mermaid Mimi," said Dreamy.

Mermaid Mimi was known for all her fancy fin twirls and backflips. She was so pretty. She wore her turquoise hair in braids that she kept pinned up in a bun, decorated with shiny pearls. Her shell top was the color of peaches, and her long scaly fins matched her hair.

"I'll see you all at the party," Mimi said in her soft, raspy voice.

The two friends were floating by Mermaid Cove when, all of a sudden, Kali could no longer see Dreamy. She began to call out to her, "Dreamy! Dreamy! Where are you?" Kali's voice was full of panic. "Dreamy, I don't like this game you're playing. It's not funny. Dreamy! Where are you?" Kali began to cry. She stumbled upon a nice spot covered in cherry blossoms and decided she would stop there to look for Dreamy. But she was nowhere to be found. Kali didn't know what to do. She was officially lost and alone.

"There, there, little one," a gentle voice whispered.

Kali jumped as somebody softly patted her on the back, not sure who it was. When she turned around, all she saw was a tiny bright pink light. But the more she stared at it, the clearer it became. It was a fairy with red glitter wings, wearing a beautiful white halo dress and striped leggings.

"Hi there, I'm Peppermint but you can call me Pep. I'm here to escort you to the dance battle party."

Pep sprinkled some fairy dust and, just like that, Kali and Pep were at the party, celebrating with all the fairytale creatures. Dreamy was already there. She introduced Kali to all her friends, and they greeted each other with warm hugs and big smiles.

"Kali, I'm sorry we got separated. I should have warned you that I am new to floating and sometimes I can't control my speed. But I sure am glad Pep got you here safely."

They all gathered around the big, round table to eat lunch, which was a covered with all their favorite fruits, cheeses and of course every sweet treat you could think of. From strawberries and lemonberries to strawberry cream cheese sugar cones, chocolates, cotton candy macarons and more.

Once they finished, they talked about what they did the past week and what they have planned for the upcoming week. And finally, they sang all the latest songs and danced to all the TikTok mashups. Kali even won the TikTok challenge competition. She was super excited! Eventually, it was time for Kali and Dreamy to go back home. Kali knew Mommy and Daddy would be waiting for them.

They said their goodbyes and then went on their way.

Kali and Dreamy were so tired that they skipped bath time and hopped right into bed, still in their BIG fluffy princess dresses and with the biggest smile on their faces.

They both fell asleep thinking about how much fun they'd had and how they couldn't wait until next Monday. It was all they dreamed about that night.

The end

But wait... there's more!

Meet the characters!

Kali
Peppermint

Dreamy

Mimi

Fun facts!

Dreamy is Kali's cute and cuddly Unicorn pet and bestfriend, who likes to:

Dance
Sing
Play with Kali
Coloring
And eat
marshmallow
pizza

Kali is an 8 year old girl who lives in Katy, Texas. She is very sweet, loves adventure and enjoys every moment with her bestie, Dreamy!
She likes to:

Skating
Selfies
Watching movies Gymnastics
And eat Lemonberries

Let's

play!

Can you help Dreamy find all the words?

Banana	Dreamy
Unicorn	Lemonberry
Pancakes	Dance
Kali	Mermaid
Princess	Fairytale

F A R O G D R I Q D Z R
A R P B A N A N A R L V
I Z R O H X R K C E Y O
R G I T D T C U M L J I
Y F N K A L O O T K E H
T R C T N H N J R A K L
A E E D C B A Q I L N G
L H S T E D R Y U I B J
E B S R O L I T H K U I
U H R T K A V A B J D L
R Y M A E R D I M T E O
K G P E U N I C O R N C
C A E N T O A R H K E T
P P A N C A K E S Q T M

Oh no!
Kali is lost.
Can you help her
find Dreamy?

Let your
imagination
lead the way.

www.ingramcontent.com/pod-product-compliance
Lightning Source LLC
Chambersburg PA
CBHW040900110726
48005CB00001B/141